To the faculty, staff, and children of Shaaray Tefila Nursery School

2015937116. ISBN 978-0-7636-7990-3. This book was typeset in Stempel Schneidler. The illustrations were hand-drawn using a Pelikan M805 fountain pen with a nib made into a "Vintage Flex" by Richard Binder. They were then hand-colored using Diamine inks and Holbein Smalt Blue gouache on Stonehenge paper.
Candlewick Press, 99 Dover Street, Somerville, Massachusetts 02144. visit us at www.candlewick.com.
Printed in Heshan, Guangdong, China. 15 16 17 18 19 20 LEO 10 9 8 7 6 5 4 3 2 1

SWAP!

STEVE LIGHT

CANDLEWICK PRESS

An old ship.

A sad friend.

One button for
two teacups.

SWAP!

Two teacups for
three coils of rope.

SWAP!

Two coils of rope
for six oars.

SWAP!

Two oars for four flags.

SWAP!

One flag for three anchors.

SWAP!

Two anchors for nine sails.

SWAP!

Two sails for
two ship's wheels.

SWAP!

One ship's wheel for three hats.

One hat for three birds.

SWAP!

One bird for
one carved figurehead.

A new ship.
A happy friend.

AHOY!